W9-BVD-975

Dear Parent:

Buckle up! You are about to join your child on a very exciting journey. The destination? Independent reading!

Road to Reading will help you and your child get there. The program offers books at five levels, or Miles, that accompany children from their first attempts at reading to successfully reading on their own. Each Mile is paved with engaging stories and delightful artwork.

Getting Started
For children who know the alphabet and are eager to begin reading
- easy words • fun rhythms • big type • picture clues

Reading With Help
For children who recognize some words and sound out others with help
- short sentences • pattern stories • simple plotlines

Reading On Your Own
For children who are ready to read easy stories by themselves
- longer sentences • more complex plotlines • easy dialogue

First Chapter Books
For children who want to take the plunge into chapter books
- bite-size chapters • short paragraphs • full-color art

Chapter Books
For children who are comfortable reading independently
- longer chapters • occasional black-and-white illustrations

There's no need to hurry through the Miles. Road to Reading is designed without age or grade levels. Children can progress at their own speed, developing confidence and pride in their reading ability no matter what their age or grade.

So sit back and enjoy the ride—every Mile of the way!

Cover photography by: Scott Fujikawa, Lin Carlson, Patrick Kittel, Vince Okada, and Lisa Collins

A GOLDEN BOOK • New York
Golden Books Publishing Company, Inc. New York, New York 10106

BARBIE and associated trademarks are owned by and used under license from Mattel, Inc. © 1999 Mattel, Inc. All rights reserved. Printed in the U.S.A. No part of this book may be copied or reproduced without written permission from the copyright owner. A GOLDEN BOOK®, GOLDEN BOOKS®, G DESIGN®, and SHIELD DESIGN™ are trademarks of Golden Books Publishing Company, Inc. Library of Congress Catalog Card Number: 98-88158

ISBN: 0-307-26326-6   A MCMXCIX

Barbie™

barbie.com:
kitty's surprise

by Barbara Richards
illustrated by S.I. International

It was the last day of school.

Michelle and Amy

could not sit still.

Amy whispered to Michelle,

"Do you want to swim

in my new pool tomorrow?"

Michelle nodded.

"I'll bring my new float,"

she whispered back.

Michelle woke up early
the next morning.
She put on her bathing suit.
She grabbed her pink towel.

Then she looked
for her float.
It was not in her toy chest.
It was not under the bed.

Michelle looked in her closet.

She didn't see her float.

But she did see

a fluffy white tail.

It was her cat, Marshmallow,

sleeping under a pile of clothes.

"Marshmallow, what is

wrong with you?"

asked Michelle.

Lately, Marshmallow

was acting very strange.

She was always sleeping.

And she was getting

fatter and fatter.

"Something is wrong
with Marshmallow.
She is getting too fat,"
Michelle told her mom.
Michelle's mother was knitting
a pair of baby booties.

"Marshmallow is fine."

Her mom laughed.

"I guess both of us

are getting fatter.

I can't wait until

the baby is born."

"Something is wrong
with Marshmallow.
She is always sleeping,"
Michelle told her dad.
He was painting
Michelle's old high chair.

"She's just tired,"
said her dad.
"Do you think

your new brother or sister
will like this color?"
Michelle rolled her eyes.
All her parents talked about
was the new baby.

Michelle found her float

in the garage.

Then she headed over to Amy's.

They dove for pennies
in the pool.
Then they did water ballet.

"This summer is
going to be the best,"
said Amy.
Michelle sighed.
"I hope so," she said.
"If only I can find out
what's wrong with Marshmallow.
She's acting very strange.
And she's fatter than ever."

Amy put her arm

around her friend.

"Did you talk to your parents?"

she asked.

"I tried," said Michelle.

"But all they care about

is the new baby."

"Let's ask Barbie!" Amy said.

"You mean go through
  my computer?" asked Michelle.

"Of course!" said Amy.

The month before,
  the girls had an amazing adventure.

They typed in *barbie.com*
  on Michelle's computer.

Suddenly, they were
  in Barbie's house!

"What a great idea," said Michelle.

"Barbie is the best
  at solving problems."

The next night,

Amy slept over

at Michelle's house.

They waited until Michelle's parents

went to bed.

Then they sneaked Marshmallow

into the computer room.

Michelle turned on the computer.

She typed *barbie.com*.

The screen turned pink.

She clicked on

Barbie's house.

Before long the screen

began to flash.

Light pink! Hot pink! Cotton-candy pink!

Then the screen began to grow.

It grew bigger and bigger.

Michelle held on tight to Marshmallow.

She and Amy stepped

into the computer.

Pink fog swirled around them.

A voice called out.

"Welcome back, girls!"

It was Barbie!

"Hi Barbie!"

said Michelle and Amy together.

Michelle put her cat down

on Barbie's pink rug.

"Who's this?" Barbie asked.

"This is my cat, Marshmallow,"

said Michelle.

"We're worried about her.

She's always sleeping.

And she's too fat."

Amy added,

"We were hoping

you could help."

"Don't worry, girls,"
said Barbie.

"I know a lot about animals.
I'm a trained veterinarian.
I'll find out what's wrong."

Barbie put her hand
on Marshmallow's round tummy.

"Maybe she swallowed
a big balloon,"
said Amy.
"Like the ones
at my birthday party."

Michelle bit her lip.

"Maybe Marshmallow is just sad,"

she said.

"Like when we found out

we wouldn't be

in the same class at school next year."

"What do you think, Barbie?"
Amy asked.

"There is nothing wrong
with this cat," said Barbie.

"Except that she is
about to have kittens!"

"Kittens!"

yelled Michelle and Amy.

They couldn't believe it!

"When will they be born?"

asked Michelle.

"Very soon," said Barbie.

Barbie placed a soft blanket

under Marshmallow.

"What can we do

to help?" asked Amy.

Barbie smiled.

"Cats don't need help

having babies.

They know just

what to do."

Barbie led the girls

out to her living room.

"So, Michelle, are you excited

about summer?"

asked Barbie.

Michelle didn't hear her.

She just stared off into space.

She was thinking

about baby kittens.

And her new baby brother or sister.

"Is something wrong?"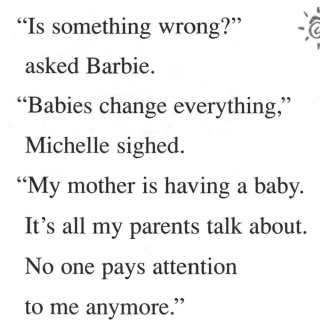
asked Barbie.

"Babies change everything,"
Michelle sighed.

"My mother is having a baby.
It's all my parents talk about.
No one pays attention
to me anymore."

Barbie gave Michelle a hug.

"Babies do change lots of things,"

said Barbie.

"But that doesn't mean

your parents don't love you."

Michelle frowned.

"But they never

have time for me,"

she complained.

"Your parents must be very busy,"
said Barbie.
"They'll be busy
after the baby comes, too.
But so will you."

"I will?" asked Michelle.

"Of course," said Barbie.

"Being a big sister is

  a very important job.

  Your parents will need your help.

  And don't forget,

  you will have someone new to love."

  Michelle grinned.

"That's true," she said.

"I'll have a new brother or sister to love.

  And the new kittens, too!

  Maybe it won't be so bad

  after all.

  Thanks, Barbie!"

Barbie looked at her watch.

"Are you ready to check

on Marshmallow now?"

she asked.

"Let's go!"

Amy and Michelle cried.

They ran into

Barbie's computer room.

Marshmallow sat in the corner—
with three tiny kittens!
The kittens made
little squeaking noises.
There were two grey ones.
And there was one white kitten
with a pink nose.

"I have an idea," said Amy.

"Let's make Marshmallow a house."

Barbie found an empty box.

Michelle drew a picture
of a door and two windows.
"I'll color it yellow," said Michelle.
"That way, it will match
the baby's new high chair."

Soon it was time to go.

Barbie turned on the computer.

She typed *michelle.com*.

Amy and Michelle hugged Barbie.

They stepped into the pink fog.

"I knew Barbie could help us,"
said Amy.
They were back
in Michelle's family room.
"Now I only have one problem,"
said Michelle.
"What will I name the kittens?"
"Let's name the grey ones
Ashes and Misty," said Amy.
"And the white kitten is so pretty,
she should have
an extra pretty name."
"I've got it!" cried Michelle.

"Welcome to the family, Barbie!"

A NOTE TO PARENTS

W9-BVE-101

Reading Aloud with Your Child

Research shows that reading books aloud is the single most valuable support parents can provide in helping children learn to read.

- Be a ham! The more enthusiasm you display, the more your child will enjoy the book.
- Run your finger underneath the words as you read to signal that the print carries the story.
- Leave time for examining the illustrations more closely; encourage your child to find things in the pictures.
- Invite your youngster to join in whenever there's a repeated phrase in the text.
- Link up events in the book with similar events in your child's life.
- If your child asks a question, stop and answer it. The book can be a means to learning more about your child's thoughts.

Listening to Your Child Read Aloud

The support of your attention and praise is absolutely crucial to your child's continuing efforts to learn to read.

- If your child is learning to read and asks for a word, give it immediately so that the meaning of the story is not interrupted. DO NOT ask your child to sound out the word.
- On the other hand, if your child initiates the act of sounding out, don't intervene.
- If your child is reading along and makes what is called a miscue, listen for the sense of the miscue. If the word "road" is substituted for the word "street," for instance, no meaning is lost. Don't stop the reading for a correction.
- If the miscue makes no sense (for example, "horse" for "house"), ask your child to reread the sentence because you're not sure you understand what's just been read.
- Above all else, enjoy your child's growing command of print and make sure you give lots of praise. *You are your child's first teacher — and the most important one. Praise from you is critical for further risk-taking and learning.*

— Priscilla Lynch
Ph.D., New York University
Educational Consultant

To my nieces Tarann and Azure
and my nephew Scyler Hawkins,
with love.

— A.S.M.

Text copyright © 1996 by Angela Shelf Medearis.
Illustrations copyright © 1996 by Maxie Chambliss.
All rights reserved. Published by Scholastic Inc.
HELLO READER!, CARTWHEEL BOOKS, and the CARTWHEEL BOOKS
logo are registered trademarks of Scholastic Inc.

No part of this publication may be reproduced in whole or in part, or stored in a
retrieval system, or transmitted in any form or by any means, electronic, mechanical,
photocopying, recording, or otherwise, without written permission of the publisher.
For information regarding permission, write to Scholastic Inc., 555 Broadway, New
York, NY 10012.

Library of Congress Cataloging-in-Publication Data

Medearis, Angela Shelf.
   Here comes the snow : by Angela Shelf Medearis ; illustrated by Maxie
Chambliss.
      p.   cm.—(Hello reader! Level 1)
   "Cartwheel Books."
   Summary: After waiting anxiously for the arrival of snow, children enjoy it by
making snow angels, throwing snowballs, and riding their sleds.
   ISBN 0-590-26266-1
   [1. Snow—Fiction. 2. Stories in rhyme.] I. Chambliss, Maxie, ill.
II. Title. III. Series.
PZ8.3.M551155He   1996
[E]—dc20   95-17364
                                                                      CIP
                                                                      AC

12 11 10 9 8 7 6   8 9/9 0 1/0

Printed in the U.S.A.   23

First Scholastic printing, January 1996

Here Comes the SNOW

by Angela Shelf Medearis
Illustrated by Maxie Chambliss

Hello Reader! — Level 1

SCHOLASTIC INC.
New York Toronto London Auckland Sydney

Coats on.

Boots on.

But no snow.

Small mittens.

Long scarves.

But no snow.

The wind howls in.
Trees sway and bend .
But no snow.

Then,
one flake, two flakes.
Here comes the snow!

Soon everything is bright
and cold and white.
Snow!

We run outside.

We slip and slide.
Snow!

Arms wave.
Our angels are made.
Snow!

Snowballs fly.
We duck and hide.
Snow!

We pat and roll
three balls of snow.
Cold ears, cold hands.

Two eyes and one nose
for the snowman.

Playtime is over.

Good-bye snow.

It's time to have some hot cocoa!